HOW THE RHINOCEROS GOT HIS SKIN

How the Rhinoceros got his Skin

Rudyard Kipling
Illustrated by Jenny Thorne

PETER BEDRICK BOOKS
NEW YORK

First American edition published in 1987 by Peter Bedrick Books 125 East
23 Street New York, NY 10010. Published by agreement with Macmillan
Children's Books, a division of Macmillan Publishers Ltd., London &
Basingstoke.

Text copyright The National Trust

Illustrations copyright © 1985 Macmillan Publishers Ltd.

Library of Congress Cataloging-in-Publication Data
   Kipling, Rudyard, 1865–1936.
      How the rhinoceros got his skin.

      (A Just so story)
      Summary: Relates how the rhinoceros's lack of manners resulted
   in his baggy skin and bad temper.
      [1. Rhinoceros—Fiction] I. Thorne, Jenny, ill. II. Title.
   PZ7.K632Hm   1987   [E]   86–28857
   ISBN 0-87226-137-9 (lib. bdg.)

Printed in Hong Kong
Reinforced binding

HOW THE RHINOCEROS GOT HIS SKIN

 ONCE upon a time, on an uninhabited island on the shores of the Red Sea, there lived a Parsee from whose hat the rays of the sun were reflected in more-than-oriental splendour. And the Parsee lived by the Red Sea with nothing but his hat and his knife and a cooking-stove of the kind that you must particularly never touch. And one day he took

flour and water and currants and plums and sugar and things, and made himself one cake which was two feet across and three feet thick. It was indeed a Superior Comestible (*that's* Magic), and he put it on the stove because *he* was allowed to cook on that stove, and he baked it and he baked it till it was all done brown and smelt most sentimental. But just as he was going to eat it

8

there came down to the beach from the Altogether
Uninhabited Interior one Rhinoceros with a horn on his
nose, two piggy eyes, and few manners. In those days
the Rhinoceros's skin fitted him quite tight. There were
no wrinkles in it anywhere. He looked exactly like a
Noah's Ark Rhinoceros, but of course much bigger. All

the same, he had no manners then, and he has no manners now, and he never will have any manners. He said, 'How!' and the Parsee left that cake and climbed to the top of a palm-tree with nothing on but his hat, from which the rays of the sun were always reflected in more-than-oriental splendour. And the Rhinoceros upset the

oil-stove with his nose, and the cake rolled on the sand, and he spiked that cake on the horn of his nose, and he ate it, and he went away, waving his tail, to the desolate and Exclusively Uninhabited Interior which abuts on the islands of Mazanderan, Socotra, and the Promontories of the Larger Equinox. Then the Parsee came down from

his palm-tree and put the stove on its legs and recited the following *Sloka*, which, as you have not heard, I will now proceed to relate:—

> *'Them that takes cakes*
> *Which the Parsee-man bakes*
> *Makes dreadful mistakes.'*

And there was a great deal more in that than you would think.

Because, five weeks later, there was a heat-wave in the Red Sea, and everybody took off all the clothes they had.

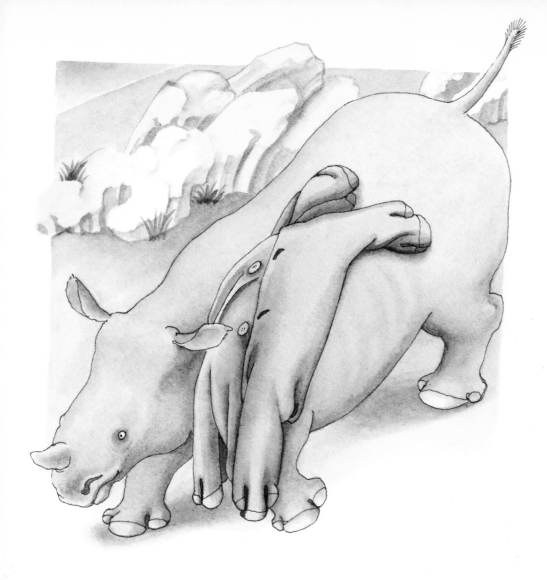

The Parsee took off his hat; but the Rhinoceros took off
his skin and carried it over his shoulder as he came down
to the beach to bathe. In those days it buttoned underneath with three buttons and looked like a waterproof.
He said nothing whatever about the Parsee's cake,
because he had eaten it all; and he never had any
manners, then, since, or henceforward. He waddled

17

straight into the water and blew bubbles through his nose, leaving his skin on the beach.

Presently the Parsee came by and found the skin, and he smiled one smile that ran all round his face two times. Then he danced three times round the skin and rubbed his hands. Then he went to his camp and filled his hat

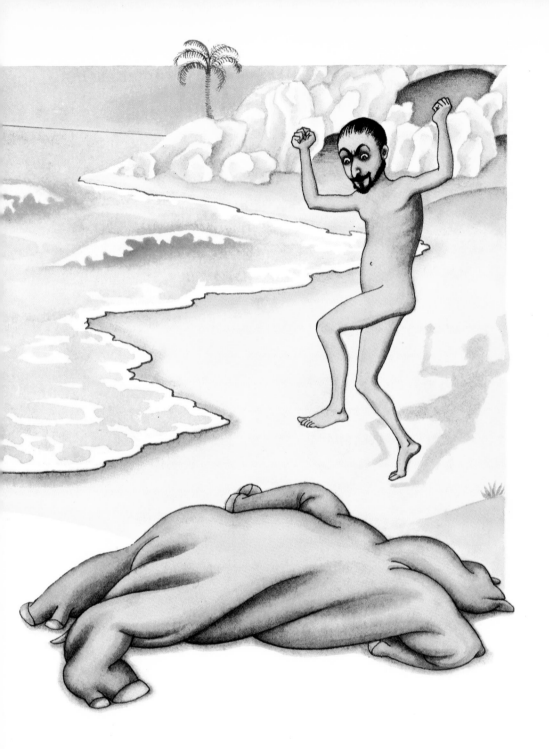

with cake-crumbs, for the Parsee never ate anything but cake, and never swept out his camp.

He took that skin,

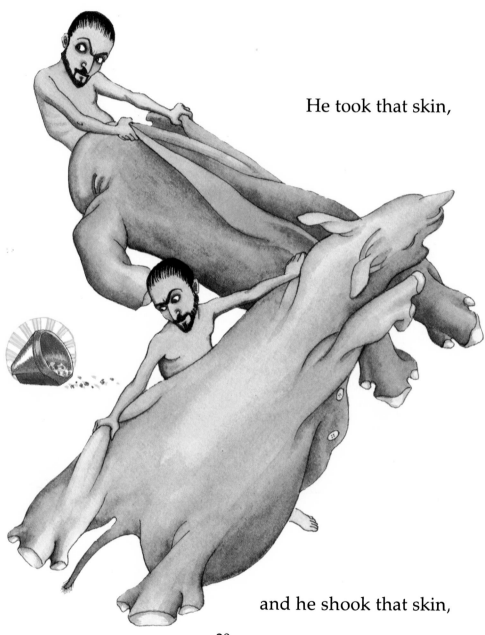

and he shook that skin,

and he scrubbed that skin, and

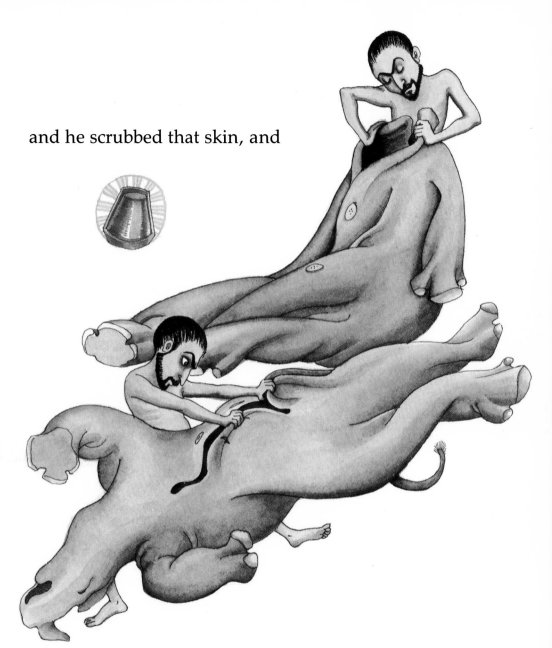

he rubbed that skin just as full of old, dry, stale, tickly cake-crumbs and some burned currants as ever it could *possibly* hold. Then he climbed to the top of his palm-tree

and waited for the Rhinoceros to come out of the water
and put it on.

And the Rhinoceros did. He buttoned it up with the three buttons, and it tickled like cake-crumbs in bed. Then he wanted to scratch, but that made it worse; and then he lay down on the sands and rolled and rolled and rolled, and every time he rolled the cake-crumbs tickled him worse and worse and worse. Then he ran to the

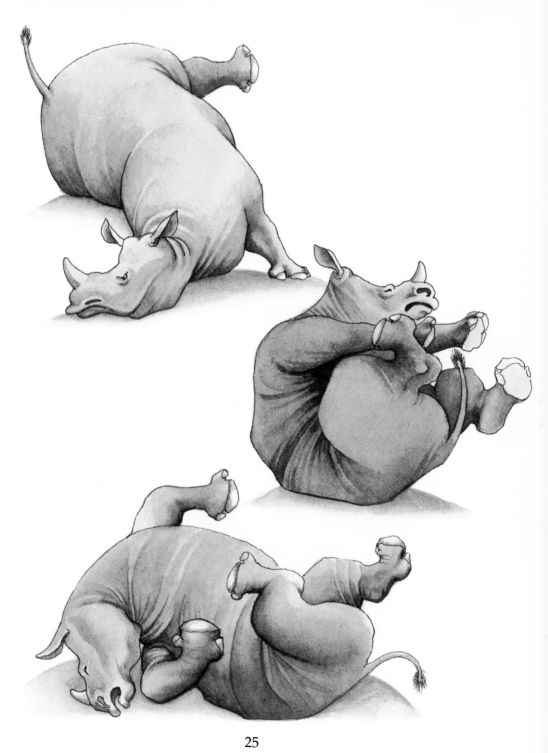

25

palm-tree and rubbed and rubbed and rubbed himself
against it. He rubbed so much and so hard that he
rubbed his skin into a great fold over his shoulders, and
another fold underneath, where the buttons used to be
(but he rubbed the buttons off), and he rubbed some
more folds over his legs. And it spoiled his temper, but it
didn't make the least difference to the cake-crumbs.

They were inside his skin and they tickled. So he went home, very angry indeed and horribly scratchy; and from that day to this every rhinoceros has great folds in his skin and a very bad temper, all on account of the cake-crumbs inside.

But the Parsee came down from his palm-tree, wearing his hat, from which the rays of the sun were reflected in more-than-oriental splendour, packed up his cooking-stove, and went away in the direction of Orotavo, Amygdala, the Upland Meadows of Ananta-rivo, and the Marshes of Sonaput.

This Uninhabited Island
　　Is off Cape Gardafui,
By the Beaches of Socotra
　　And the Pink Arabian Sea:
But it's hot—too hot from Suez
　　For the likes of you and me
　　　　Ever to go
　　　　In a P. and O.
And call on the Cake-Parsee!